Other Books by JENNIFER BARTOLI
Snow on Bear's Nose
The Story of the Grateful Crane

An Albert Whitman
International Picture Book

Jennifer Bartoli

IN A MEADOW, TWO HARES HIDE

Illustrated by
Takeo Ishida

Albert Whitman & Company, Chicago

In a meadow, it was morning.
The tall grass shone in the early sun.

A young hare hopped about the field.
Her name was Mimo.
She was hungry, and it was time to look for food.

Here she found the last of the summer's
wild grapes. They were wet and sweet.

Mimo ate many of the dark grapes.
Then she hid in the shadow of the vine
and watched the meadow around her.

Down a small grassy hill something moved.
Mimo sat up, ready to leap away.
Her nose twitching, she looked again.

Coming toward her was another young hare,
all brown and white and furry.

Deep in the sunny grass,
the two hares looked at each other.

Lepo, the other hare, put out a paw.
Mimo's long ears went straight back.

But suddenly Mimo's ears were up again.
She sniffed the cool wind.
Quickly she sprang into the air.

Lepo heard something, too.
He turned toward the woods.
There, only the tips of two pointed ears
showed above the grass.

Into the meadow a fox had come.
And when the fox saw Mimo and Lepo,
the chase was on!

The two hares ran,
turning and darting to escape the fox.
Their two white tails
        bobbed up and down in the grass,
                and the fox followed them.

Mimo could feel the fox behind her.
It was coming closer and closer.

Ahead she saw a thicket of sharp branches
hanging low over the grass.
She raced under them to safety.

The fox was fast, but so was Mimo.

Once more the meadow was quiet.
One dark eye peeked out from the thicket.
Mimo was safe now. The fox had gone.

But where was Lepo?
Mimo sniffed the air and listened for him.
The grass was still. She could not smell him.

Mimo was alone.

Slowly the warm days of autumn ended,
and winter settled over the meadow.
Mimo's fur grew thick to keep her warm.
It was white now, to match the quiet snow.
Only the tips of her ears were dark.

Mimo was always hungry.
But she looked for food only at night
or in the safe darkness of early morning.

When light filled the sky,
Mimo hid in her home in the snow.

Early one morning, Mimo came to a path
of new tracks on top of the snow.
First she touched the tracks with her nose.
Then she raised her head and listened to the wind.

These were Lepo's tracks—she could tell.
In front of her stood a winding line of trees.
Lepo had gone around them. There were his tracks.

Mimo followed the tracks
            and hopped around the trees, too.

Beyond the trees, Lepo was looking for food
in the snowy field.
Suddenly an eagle flew across the morning sky.
Lepo heard its wings. He looked up.

The eagle saw him. Where could Lepo go?

Lepo turned, the sun and the eagle behind him,
and raced zig-zag across the meadow.

Snow sprayed upon snow and made
a fine white trail where Lepo ran.

The eagle swept closer.

Suddenly, out of the whiteness all around,
jumped Mimo.
Eagles and hares screeched in the cold, quiet air.

With her strong hind legs, Mimo kicked the eagle.
The eagle slipped. Its sharp claws dug into the snow.

Mimo and Lepo ran. This was their chance to escape.

In seconds the eagle was up.
It flew in great circles over the meadow.
But already Lepo and Mimo were far away.

The two hares ran until they came to a clump
of green bamboo growing in the snow.
Here was food for them and a place to hide.

And here Mimo and Lepo could rest at last.
Now they were safe and together.

HARES

Lepo and Mimo are hares, furry animals with long ears, short bushy tails, and strong hind legs. Although they look like rabbits, hares are bigger and usually have longer ears. Some hares grow to be twenty-five inches or sixty-four centimeters long, while a large adult wild rabbit may reach a length of fourteen inches or thirty-six centimeters. The North American jack rabbit and the snowshoe rabbit are really hares, not rabbits.

Hares are found over most of the world. Like Lepo and Mimo, many hares have brown fur that is shed and replaced with a coat of white in the winter. Other hares have buff-colored or gray fur, and some have fur that stays white all year round.

Rabbits live in burrows, but hares use the weight of their bodies to make nests in the grass and weeds. These nests are called "forms." Hares eat plants, searching for food only at night and returning to their forms at day-break.

Hares have only weak black-and-white vision, but they can hear and smell very well. These keen senses help them evade natural enemies like the fox and the eagle. Hares also escape predators by running with great speed and suddenly "jinking," jerking quickly to change direction. Hares make screeching noises, and they can stamp their hind legs to warn of danger. If necessary, hares will even swim to safety.

Baby hares are called "leverets." Unlike baby rabbits, they are born with fur and with their eyes open. These tiny newborn animals can hop about immediately, and they soon make their own forms in the grass. The mother or doe hare then comes to feed them individually.

Jennifer Bartoli

Jennifer Bartoli is a Chicago writer who in this book, as in Snow on Bear's Nose, *demonstrates her ability to tell an engaging animal story without implying human characteristics and motivations. As the mother of Pietro and Amelia, and as a former editor of children's books, Mrs. Bartoli brings special sensitivity to her writing. Her picture book* The Story of the Grateful Crane *is a Japanese folktale retold with dignity and simplicity. In* Nonna, *she deals with the death of a special grandmother.*

Takeo Ishida

Takeo Ishida is a well-known Japanese artist whose illustrations beautifully capture the natural world. In Snow on Bear's Nose, *also published by Albert Whitman, mischievous Japanese moon-bears delight the imagination. Takeo Ishida's fresh colors and delicate perceptions combine in art that is appealing for all ages.*

Library of Congress Cataloging in Publication Data

Bartoli, Jennifer.
  In a meadow, two hares hide.

  (International picture books)
  SUMMARY: Two young hares living in a meadow survive
the changing seasons and their natural enemies.
  [1. Hares—Legends and stories.   2. Hares—Fiction]
I. Ishida, Takeo, 1922-   II. Title.   III. Series.
PZ10.3.B285In   [E]   78-15221
ISBN 0-8075-3628-8

Text © 1978 by Jennifer Bartoli. Illustrations © Gakken Co., Ltd., 1975.
By arrangement with Gakken Co., Ltd., and Mark Paterson, Colchester, U.K.
Published simultaneously in Canada by George J. McLeod, Limited, Toronto.